LITTLE HEDGEHOG
BOOKS

VISIT AMAZON.COM FOR MORE
LITTLE HEDGEHOG BOOKS

GRAMMIESAURUS AND ME

When we are together, we like to act silly and stomp around.

Grammiesaurus is always impressed by my loud roar... even when I'm a little *too* loud.

She likes to brag about me to her friends at the watering hole.

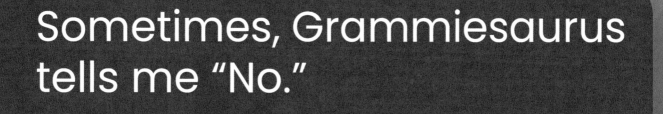

Sometimes, Grammiesaurus tells me "No."

But I know that it's only to keep me safe.

TAR PIT

Food just tastes better when Grammiesaurus makes it for me.

At the beach, she makes me wear a hat so I don't get sunburned. (But she wears one too.)

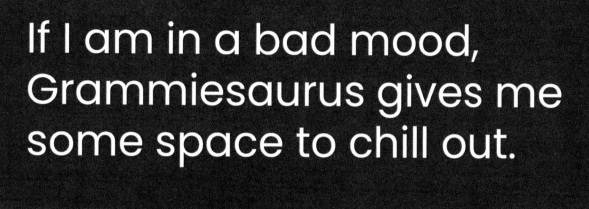

If I am in a bad mood, Grammiesaurus gives me some space to chill out.

She worries when I try new things, but she knows that I need to soar when the time is right.

When Grammiesaurus tucks me in for the night, I feel safe and snuggly because I know she's near me.

Made in the USA
Las Vegas, NV
15 December 2024

14308469R00021